Runny Honey

 **Crabtree Publishing Company**
www.crabtreebooks.com

PMB16A, 350 Fifth Avenue
Suite 3308,
New York, NY

616 Welland Avenue
St. Catharines, ON
L2M 5V6

Published by Crabtree Publishing in 2008

First published in 2007 by
Franklin Watts
(A division of Hachette Children's Books)
338 Euston Road
London   NW1 3BH

Text © Jane Clarke 2007
Illustration © Tomislav Zlatic 2007

Cataloging-in-Publication data is available at the Library of Congress.

ISBN 978-0-7787-3862-6 (rlb)
ISBN 978-0-7787-3893-0 (pbk)

Series Editor: Jackie Hamley
Series Advisor: Dr Hilary Minns
Series Designer: Peter Scoulding

Printed in the U.S.A.

Runny Honey

by Jane Clarke

Illustrated by Tomislav Zlatic

Crabtree Publishing Company

www.crabtreebooks.com

Jane Clarke

"I love eating runny honey on buttered toast, but I would never stick my nose in the jar!"

Tomislav Zlatic

"I started liking honey when I was very young. It's funny, but when you start to mess with it, you just can't get rid of it. It's so sticky!"

Runny honey!
Yummy! Yummy!

Runny honey
on Bear's paws.

Runny honey
in Bear's jaws.

Runny honey in
Bear's tummy.

Runny honey!
Yummy! Yummy!

Runny honey
on Bear's nose.

Runny honey
on Bear's toes.

Runny honey
everywhere!
On the table,
on the chair ...

on the walls ...

on the floor ...

on the windows ...

and on the door.

17

Runny honey
in Bear's hair.

18

Runny honey everywhere!

Runny honey
in Bear's pants.

Run, Bear, run!
Here come the ...

... ANTS!

Notes for adults

TADPOLES are structured to provide support for early readers. The stories may also be used by adults for sharing with young children.

Starting to read alone can be daunting. **TADPOLES** help by providing visual support and repeating high frequency words and phrases. These books will both develop confidence and encourage reading and rereading for pleasure.

If you are reading this book with a child, here are a few suggestions:

1. Make reading fun! Choose a time to read when you and the child are relaxed and have time to share the story.
2. Talk about the story before you start reading. Look at the cover and the blurb. What might the story be about? Why might the child like it?
3. Encourage the child to reread the story, and to retell the story in their own words, using the illustrations to remind them what has happened.
4. Discuss the story and see if the child can relate it to their own experiences, or perhaps compare it to another story they know.
5. Give praise! Children learn best in a positive environment.